SCOTT-KING'S
MODERN EUROPE

SCOTT-KING'S MODERN EUROPE

by Evelyn Waugh

CHAPMAN & HALL

MCMXLVII

MARIÆ IMMACULATÆ ANTONIÆ
CONIUGIS PRUDENTIORIS
AUDACI CONIUGI

IN 1946 Scott-King had been classical master at Granchester for twenty-one years. He was himself a Granchesterian and had returned straight from the University after failing for a fellowship. There he had remained, growing slightly bald and slightly corpulent, known to generations of boys first as 'Scottie,' then of late years, while barely middle-aged, as 'old Scottie'; a school 'institution,' whose precise and slightly nasal lamentations of modern decadence were widely parodied.

Granchester is not the most illustrious of English public schools but it is, or, as Scott-King would maintain, was, entirely respectable ; it plays an annual cricket match at Lord's ; it numbers a dozen or so famous men among its old boys, who, in general, declare without apology : ' I was at Granchester ' —unlike the sons of lesser places who are apt to say : ' As a matter of fact I was at a place called——. You see at the time my father . . .'

When Scott-King was a boy and when he first returned as a master, the school was almost equally divided into a Classical and a Modern Side, with a group of negligible and neglected specialists called ' the Army Class.' Now the case was altered and out of 450 boys scarcely 50 read Greek. Scott-King had watched his classical colleagues fall away one by one, some to rural rectories, some to the British Council and the B.B.C., to be replaced by physicists and economists from the provincial universities, until now, instead of inhabiting solely the rare intellectual atmosphere of the Classical Sixth, he was obliged to descend for many periods a week to cram lower boys with Xenophon and Sallust. But Scott-King did not repine. On the contrary he found a peculiar relish in contemplating the victories of barbarism and positively rejoiced in his reduced station, for he was of a type, unknown in the New World but quite

2

common in Europe, which is fascinated by obscurity and failure.

'Dim' is the epithet for Scott-King and it was a fellow-feeling, a blood-brotherhood in dimness, which first drew him to study the works of the poet Bellorius.

No one, except perhaps Scott-King himself, could be dimmer. When, poor and in some discredit, Bellorius died in 1646 in his native town of what was then a happy kingdom of the Habsburg Empire and is now the turbulent modern state of Neutralia,[1] he left as his life's work a single folio volume containing a poem of some 1500 lines of Latin hexameters. In his lifetime the only effect of the publication was to annoy the Court and cause his pension to be cancelled. After his death it was entirely forgotten until the middle of the last century when it was reprinted in Germany in a collection of late Renaissance texts. It was in this edition that Scott-King found it during a holiday on the Rhine, and at once his heart stirred with the recognition of kinship. The subject was irredeemably tedious—a visit to an imaginary island of the New World where in primitive simplicity, untainted by tyranny or dogma, there subsisted a virtuous, chaste and reasonable community. The lines were

[1] The Republic of Neutralia is imaginary and composite and represents no existing state.

3

correct and melodious, enriched by many happy figures of speech ; Scott-King read them on the deck of the river steamer as vine and turret, cliff and terrace and park, swept smoothly past. How they offended—by what intended or unintended jab of satire, blunted today ; by what dangerous speculation—is not now apparent. That they should have been forgotten is readily intelligible to anyone acquainted with the history of Neutralia.

Something must be known of this history if we are to follow Scott-King with understanding. Let us eschew detail and observe that for three hundred years since Bellorius's death his country has suffered every conceivable ill the body politic is heir to. Dynastic wars, foreign invasion, disputed successions, revolting colonies, endemic syphilis, impoverished soil, masonic intrigues, revolutions, restorations, cabals, juntas, pronunciamentos, liberations, constitutions, *coups d'état*, dictatorships, assassinations, agrarian reforms, popular elections, foreign intervention, repudiation of loans, inflations of currency, trades unions, massacres, arson, atheism, secret societies—make the list full, slip in as many personal foibles as you will, you will find all these in the last three centuries of Neutralian history. Out of it emerged the present republic of Neutralia, a typical modern state, governed by a single party, acclaim-

4

ing a dominant Marshal, supporting a vast ill-paid bureaucracy whose work is tempered and humanised by corruption. This you must know ; also that the Neutralians being a clever Latin race are little given to hero-worship and make considerable fun of their Marshal behind his back. In one thing only did he earn their full-hearted esteem. He kept out of the second World War. Neutralia sequestered herself and, from having been the cockpit of factious sympathies, became remote, unconsidered, *dim* ; so that, as the face of Europe coarsened and the war, as it appeared in the common-room newspapers and the common-room wireless, cast its heroic and chivalrous disguise and became a sweaty tug-of-war between teams of indistinguishable louts, Scott-King, who had never set foot there, became Neutralian in his loyalty and as an act of homage resumed with fervour the task on which he had intermittently worked, the translation of Bellorius into Spenserian stanzas. The work was finished at the time of the Normandy landings —translation, introduction, notes. He sent it to the Oxford University Press. It came back to him. He put it away in a drawer of the pitch-pine desk in his smoky gothic study above the Granchester quadrangle. He did not repine. It was his opus, his monument to dimness.

But still the shade of Bellorius stood at his elbow demanding placation. There was unfinished business between these two. You cannot keep close company with a man, even though he be dead three centuries, without incurring obligations. Therefore at the time of the peace celebrations Scott-King distilled his learning and wrote a little essay, 4000 words long, entitled *The Last Latinist*, to commemorate the coming tercentenary of Bellorius's death. It appeared in a learned journal. Scott-King was paid twelve guineas for this fruit of fifteen years' devoted labour ; six of them he paid in income tax ; with six he purchased a large gunmetal watch which worked irregularly for a month or two and then finally failed. There the matter might well have ended.

These, then, in a general, distant view, are the circumstances — Scott - King's history ; Bellorius ; the history of Neutralia ; the year of Grace 1946— all quite credible, quite humdrum, which together produced the odd events of Scott-King's summer holiday. Let us now ' truck ' the camera forward and see him ' close-up.' You have heard all about Scott-King but you have not yet met him.

Meet him, then, at breakfast on a bleak morning at the beginning of the summer term. Unmarried assistant masters at Granchester enjoyed the use of

6

a pair of collegiate rooms in the school buildings and took their meals in the common-room. Scott-King came from his class-room where he had been taking early school, with his gown flowing behind him and a sheaf of fluttering exercise papers in his numb fingers. There had been no remission of war-time privations at Granchester. The cold grate was used as ash-tray and waste-paper basket and was rarely emptied. The breakfast-table was a litter of small pots, each labelled with a master's name, containing rations of sugar, margarine and a spurious marmalade. The breakfast dish was a slop of 'dried' eggs. Scott-King turned sadly from the sideboard. 'Anyone,' he said, ' is welcome to my share in this triumph of modern science.'

'Letter for you, Scottie,' said one of his colleagues. ' " The Honourable Professor Scott-King Esquire." Congratulations.'

It was a large, stiff envelope, thus oddly addressed, emblazoned on the flap with a coat of arms. Inside was a card and a letter. The card read : *His Magnificence the Very Reverend the Rector of the University of Simona and the Committee of the Bellorius Tercentenary Celebration Association request the honour of Professor Scott-King's assistance at the public acts to be held at Simona on July 28th– August 5th, 1946. R.S.V.P. His Excellency Dr.*

Bogdan Antonic, international secretary of the Committee, Simona University, Neutralia.

The letter was signed by the Neutralian Ambassador to the Court of St. James's. It announced that a number of distinguished scholars were assembling from all over the world to do honour to the illustrious Neutralian political thinker Bellorius and delicately intimated that the trip would be without expense on the part of the guests.

Scott-King's first thought on reading the communication was that he was the victim of a hoax. He looked round the table expecting to surprise a glance of complicity between his colleagues, but they appeared to be busy with their own concerns. Second thoughts convinced him that this sumptuous embossing and engraving was beyond their resources. The thing was authentic, then ; but Scott-King was not pleased. He felt, rather, that a long-standing private intimacy between himself and Bellorius was being rudely disturbed. He put the envelope into his pocket, ate his bread and margarine, and presently made ready for morning chapel. He stopped at the secretary's office to purchase a packet of crested school writing paper on which to inscribe ' *Mr. Scott-King regrets . . .*'

For the strange thing is that Scott-King was definitely blasé. Something of the kind has been

8

hinted before, yet, seeing him cross the quadrangle to the chapel steps, middle - aged, shabby, unhonoured and unknown, his round and learned face puckered against the wind, you would have said : ' There goes a man who has missed all the compensations of life—and knows it.' But that is because you do not yet know Scott-King ; no voluptuary surfeited by conquest, no colossus of the drama bruised and rent by doting adolescents, not Alexander, nor Talleyrand, was more blasé than Scott-King. He was an adult, an intellectual, a classical scholar, almost a poet ; he was travel-worn in the large periphery of his own mind, jaded with accumulated experience of his imagination. He was older, it might have been written, than the rocks on which he sat ; older, anyway, than his stall in chapel ; he had died many times, had Scott-King, had dived deep, had trafficked for strange webs with Eastern merchants. And all this had been but the sound of lyres and flutes to him. Thus musing, he left the chapel and went to his class-room, where for the first hours he had the lowest set.

They coughed and sneezed. One, more ingenious than the rest, attempted at length to draw him out as, it was known, he might sometimes be drawn : ' Please, sir, Mr. Griggs says it's a pure waste of our time learning classics,' but Scott-King merely replied : ' It's a waste of time coming to me and *not* learning them.'

After Latin gerunds they stumbled through half a page of Thucydides. He said : ' These last episodes of the siege have been described as tolling like a great bell,' at which a chorus rose from the back bench ' The bell ? Did you say it was the bell, sir ? ' and books were noisily shut. ' There are another twenty minutes. I said the book tolled like a bell.'

' Please, sir, I don't quite get that, sir, how can a book be like a bell, sir ? '

' If you wish to talk, Ambrose, you can start construing.'

' Please, sir, that's as far as I got, sir.'

' Has anyone done any more ? ' (Scott-King still attempted to import into the lower school the adult politeness of the Classical Sixth.) ' Very well, then, you can all spend the rest of the hour preparing the next twenty lines.'

Silence, of a sort, reigned. There was a low muttering from the back of the room, a perpetual shuffling and snuffling, but no one spoke directly to Scott-King. He gazed through the leaded panes to the leaden sky. He could hear through the wall behind him the strident tones of Griggs, the civics master, extolling the Tolpuddle martyrs. Scott-

King put his hand in his coat-pocket and felt the crisp edges of the Neutralian invitation.

He had not been abroad since 1939. He had not tasted wine for a year, and he was filled, suddenly, with deep home-sickness for the South. He had not often nor for long visited those enchanted lands ; a dozen times perhaps, for a few weeks—for one year in total of his forty-three years of life —but his treasure and his heart lay buried there. Hot oil and garlic and spilled wine ; luminous pinnacles above a dusky wall ; fireworks at night, fountains at noonday ; the impudent, inoffensive hawkers of lottery tickets moving from table to table on to the crowded pavement ; the shepherd's pipe on the scented hillside—all that travel agent ever sought to put in a folder, fumed in Scott-King's mind that drab morning. He had left his coin in the waters of Trevi ; he had wedded the Adriatic ; he was a Mediterranean man.

In the mid-morning break, on the crested school paper, he wrote his acceptance of the Neutralian invitation. That evening, and on many subsequent evenings, the talk in the common-room was about plans for the holidays. All despaired of getting abroad ; all save Griggs who was cock-a-hoop about an International Rally of Progressive Youth Leadership in Prague to which he had got himself appointed. Scott-King said nothing even when Neutralia was mentioned.

'I'd like to go somewhere I could get a decent meal,' said one of his colleagues. 'Ireland or Neutralia, or somewhere like that.'

'They'd never let you into Neutralia,' said Griggs. 'Far too much to hide. They've got teams of German physicists making atomic bombs.'

'Civil war raging.'

'Half the population in concentration camps.'

'No decent-minded man would go to Neutralia.'

'Or to Ireland for that matter,' said Griggs.

And Scott-King sat tight.

SOME weeks later Scott-King sat in the aerodrome waiting-room. His overcoat lay across his knees, his hand luggage at his feet. A loud-speaker, set high out of harm's way in the dun concrete wall, discoursed dance music and official announcements. This room, like all the others to which he had been driven in the course of the morning, was sparsely furnished and indifferently clean ; on its walls, sole concession to literary

13

curiosity, hung commendations of government savings bonds and precautions against gas attack. Scott-King was hungry, weary and dispirited for he was new to the amenities of modern travel.

He had left his hotel in London at seven o'clock that morning ; it was now past noon and he was still on English soil. He had not been ignored. He had been shepherded in and out of charabancs and offices like an idiot child ; he had been weighed and measured like a load of merchandise ; he had been searched like a criminal ; he had been cross-questioned about his past and his future, the state of his health and of his finances, as though he were applying for permanent employment of a confidential nature. Scott-King had not been nurtured in luxury and privilege, but this was not how he used to travel. And he had eaten nothing except a piece of flaccid toast and margarine in his bedroom. The ultimate asylum where he now sat proclaimed itself on the door as ' For the use of V.I.P.s only.'

' V.I.P. ? ' he asked their conductress.

She was a neat, impersonal young woman, part mid-wife, part governess, part shop-walker, in manner. 'Very Important Persons,' she replied without evident embarrassment.

' But is it all right for me to be here ? '

' It is essential.   You are a V.I.P.'

14

I wonder, thought Scott-King, how they treat quite ordinary, unimportant people ?

There were two fellow-travellers, male and female, similarly distinguished, both bound for Bellacita, capital city of Neutralia ; both, it presently transpired, guests of the Bellorius Celebration Committee.

The man was a familiar type to Scott-King ; his name Whitemaid, his calling academic, a dim man like himself, much of an age with him.

' Tell me,' said Whitemaid, ' tell me frankly '— and he looked furtive as men do when they employ that ambiguous expression—' have you ever heard of the worthy Bellorius ? '

' I know his work. I have seldom heard it discussed.'

' Ah, well, of course, he's not in my subject. I'm Roman Law,' said Whitemaid, with an accession of furtiveness that took all grandiosity from the claim. ' They asked the Professor of Poetry, you know, but he couldn't get away. Then they tried the Professor of Latin. He's red. Then they asked for anyone to represent the University. No one else was enthusiastic so I put myself forward. I find expeditions of this kind highly diverting. You are familiar with them ? '

' No.'

15

'I went to Upsala last vacation and ate very passable caviare twice a day for a week. Neutralia is not known for delicate living, alas, but one may count on rude plenty—and, of course, wine.'

'It's all a racket, anyhow,' said the third Very Important Person.

This was a woman no longer very young. Her name, Scott-King and Whitemaid had learned through hearing it frequently called through the loudspeaker and seeing it chalked on blackboards, calling her to receive urgent messages at every stage of their journey, was Miss Bombaum. It was a name notorious to almost all the world except, as it happened, to Scott-King and Whitemaid. She was far from dim ; once a roving, indeed a dashing, reporter who in the days before the war had popped up wherever there was unpleasantness— Danzig, the Alcazar, Shanghai, Wal-Wal ; now a columnist whose weekly articles were syndicated in the popular press of four continents. Scott-King did not read such articles and he had wondered idly at frequent intervals during the morning what she could be. She did not look a lady ; she did not even look quite respectable, but he could not reconcile her typewriter with the callings of actress or courtesan ; nor for that matter the sharp little sexless face under the too feminine hat and the

16

lavish style of hair-dressing. He came near the truth in suspecting her of being, what he had often heard of but never seen in the life, a female novelist.

'It's all a racket,' said Miss Bombaum, 'of the Neutralian Propaganda Bureau. I reckon they feel kind of left out of things now the war's over and want to make some nice new friends among the United Nations. We're only part of it. They've got a religious pilgrimage and a Congress of Physical Culture and an International Philatelists' Convention and heaven knows what else. I reckon there's a story in it—in Neutralia, I mean ; not in Bellorius, of course, he's been done.'

'Done ? '

'Yes, I've a copy somewhere,' she said, rummaging in her bag. 'Thought it might come in useful for the speeches.'

'You don't think,' said Scott-King, 'that we are in danger of being required to make speeches ? '

'I can't think what else we've been asked for,' said Miss Bombaum. 'Can you ? '

'I made three long speeches at Upsala,' said Whitemaid. 'They were ecstatically received.'

'Oh, dear, and I have left all my papers at home.'

'Borrow this any time you like,' said Miss Bombaum, producing Mr. Robert Graves's *Count Belisarius*. 'It's sad though. He ends up blind.'

17

The music suddenly ceased and a voice said : 'Passengers for Bellacita will now proceed to Exit D. Passengers for Bellacita will now proceed to Exit D,' while, simultaneously, the conductress appeared in the door-way and said : 'Follow me, please. Have your embarkation papers, medical cards, customs clearance slips, currency control vouchers, passports, tickets, identity dockets, travel orders, emigration certificates, baggage checks and security sheets ready for inspection at the barrier, please.'

The Very Important Persons followed her out, mingled with the less important persons who had been waiting in a nearby room, stepped into a dusty gale behind the four spinning screws of the aeroplane, mounted the step-ladder and were soon strapped into their seats as though waiting the attention of the dentist. A steward gave them brief instructions in the case of their being forced down over the sea and announced : 'We shall arrive at Bellacita at sixteen hours Neutralian time.'

'An appalling thought occurs to me,' said White-maid, 'can this mean we get no luncheon ? '

'They eat very late in Neutralia, I believe.'

'Yes, but four o'clock ! '

'I'm sure they will have arranged something for us.'

'I pray they have.'

Something had been arranged but not a luncheon. The Very Important Persons stepped out some hours later into the brilliant sunshine of Bellacita airport and at once found their hands shaken in swift succession by a deputation of their hosts. ' I bid you welcome to the land of Bellorius,' said their spokesman.

His name, he told them with a neat bow, was Arturo Fe ; his rank Doctor of Bellacita University ; but there was nothing academic in his appearance. Rather, Scott-King thought, he might be a slightly ageing film actor. He had thin, calligraphic moustaches, a hint of side-whisker, sparse but well-ordered hair, a gold-rimmed monocle, three gold teeth, and neat, dark clothes.

' Madam,' he said, ' gentlemen, your luggage will be cared for. The motor-cars await you. Come with me. Passports ? Papers ? Do not give them a thought. Everything is arranged. Come.'

At this stage Scott-King became aware of a young woman standing stolidly among them. He had taken notice of her in London where she had towered some six inches above the heads of the crowd.

' I come,' she said.

Dr. Fe bowed. ' Fe,' he said.

' Sveningen,' she answered.

'You are one of us ? Of the Bellorius Association ? ' asked Dr. Fe.

'I speak not English well. I come.'

Dr. Fe tried her in Neutralian, French, Italian and German. She replied in her own remote Nordic tongue. Dr. Fe raised hands and eyes in a pantomime of despair.

'You speak much English. I speak little English. So we speak English, yes ? I come.'

'You come ? ' said Dr. Fe.

'I come.'

'We are honoured,' said Dr. Fe.

He led them between flowering oleanders and borders of camomile, past shaded café tables at which Whitemaid longingly looked, through the airport vestibule to the glass doors beyond.

Here there was a hitch. Two sentries, shabbily uniformed but armed for action, war-worn, it seemed, but tigers for duty, barred their passage. Dr. Fe tried a high hand, he tried charm, he offered them cigarettes ; suddenly a new side of his character was revealed ; he fell into demoniac rage, he shook his fists, he bared his chryselephantine teeth, he narrowed his eyes to mongol slits of hate ; what he said was unintelligible to Scott-King but it was plainly designed to wound. The men stood firm.

Then, as suddenly as it had arisen, the squall

passed. He turned to his guests. 'Excuse one moment,' he said. 'These stupid fellows do not understand their orders. It will be arranged by the officer.' He despatched an underling.

'We box the rude mens?' suggested Miss Sveningen, moving cat-like towards the soldiers.

'No. Forgive them I beg you. They think it their duty.'

'Such little men should be polite,' said the giantess.

The officer came ; the doors flew open ; the soldiers did something with their tommy-guns which passed as a salute. Scott-King raised his hat as the little party swept out into the blaze of sunshine to the waiting cars.

'This superb young creature,' said Scott-King, 'would you say she was a slightly incongruous figure ?'

'I find her eminently, transcendently congruous,' said Whitemaid. 'I exult in her.'

Dr. Fe gallantly took the ladies under his own charge. Scott-King and Whitemaid rode with an underling. They bowled along through the suburbs of Bellacita ; tram-lines, half-finished villas, a rush of hot wind, a dazzle of white concrete. At first, when they were fresh from the upper air, the heat had been agreeable ; now his skin began to prick and tickle and Scott-King realised that he was unsuitably dressed.

'Exactly ten hours and a half since I had anything to eat,' said Whitemaid.

The underling leaned towards them from the front seat and pointed out places of interest. 'Here,' he said, 'the anarchists shot General Cardenas. Here syndico-radicals shot the auxiliary bishop. Here the Agrarian League buried alive ten Teaching Brothers. Here the bimetallists committed unspeakable atrocities on the wife of Senator Mendoza.'

'Forgive me for interrupting you,' said Whitemaid, 'but could you tell us where we are going?'

'To the Ministry. They are all happy to meet you.'

'And we are happy to meet them. But just at the moment my friend and I are rather hungry.'

'Yes,' said the underling with compassion. 'We have heard of it in our papers. Your rations in England, your strikes. Here things are very expensive but there is plenty for all who pay, so our people do not strike but work hard to become rich. It is better so, no?'

'Perhaps. We must have a talk about it some time. But at the moment it is not so much the general economic question as a personal immediate need——'

'We arrive,' said the underling. 'Here is the Ministry.'

Like much modern Neutralian building the Ministry was unfinished, but it was conceived in severe one-party style. A portico of unembellished columns, a vast, blank door-way, a bas-relief symbolising Revolution and Youth and Technical Progress and the National Genius. Inside, a staircase. On the staircase was a less predictable feature ; ranged on either side like playing-cards, like a startling hand composed entirely of Kings and Knaves, stood ascending ranks of trumpeters aged from 60 to 16, dressed in the tabards of medieval heralds ; more than this they wore blond bobbed wigs ; more than this their cheeks were palpably rouged. As Scott-King and Whitemaid set foot on the lowest step these figures of fantasy raised their trumpets to their lips and sounded a flourish, while one who might from his extreme age have been father to them all, rattled in a feeble way on a little kettle-drum. 'Frankly,' said Whitemaid, 'I am not in good heart for this kind of thing.'

They mounted between the blaring ranks, were greeted on the piano nobile by a man in plain evening-dress, and led to the reception hall which with its pews and thrones had somewhat the air of a court of law and was in fact not infrequently used

23

for condemning aspiring politicians to exile on one or other of the inhospitable islands that lay off the coast of the country.

Here they found an assembly. Under a canopy, on the central throne, sat the Minister of Rest and Culture, a saturnine young man who had lost most of his fingers while playing with a bomb during the last revolution. Scott-King and Whitemaid were presented to him by Dr. Fe. He smiled rather horribly and extended a maimed hand. Half a dozen worthies stood round him. Dr. Fe introduced them. Honorific titles, bows, smiles, shakes of the hand ; then Scott-King and Whitemaid were led to their stalls amid their fellow-guests, now about twelve in number. In each place, on the red-plush seat, lay a little pile of printed matter. ' Not precisely esculent,' said Whitemaid. Trumpets and drum sounded without ; another and final party arrived and was presented ; then the proceedings began.

The Minister of Rest and Culture had a voice, never soft perhaps, now roughened by a career of street-corner harangues. He spoke at length and was succeeded by the venerable Rector of Bella-cita University. Meanwhile Scott-King studied the books and leaflets provided for him, lavish productions of the Ministry of Popular Enlightenment—

selected speeches by the Marshal, a monograph on Neutralian pre-History, an illustrated guide to the ski-ing resorts of the country, the annual report of the Corporation of Viticulture. Nothing seemed to have bearing upon the immediate situation except one, a polyglot programme of the coming celebrations. ' *17.00 hrs.*,' he read. ' *Inauguration of the Ceremonies by the Minister of Rest and Culture. 18.00 hrs. Reception of delegates at the University of Bellacita. Official dress. 19.30 hrs. Vin d'honneur offered to the delegates by the Municipality of Bellacita. 21.00 hrs. Banquet offered by the Committee of the Bellorius Tercentenary Committee. Music by Bellacita Philharmonic Youth Squadron. Evening dress. Delegates will spend the night at the Hôtel 22nd March.*'

' Look,' said Whitemaid, ' nothing to eat until nine o'clock and, mark my words, they will be late.'

' In Neutralia,' said Dr. Arturo Fe, ' in Neutralia, when we are happy, we take no account of time. Today we are *very* happy.'

The Hôtel 22nd March was the name, derived from some forgotten event in the Marshal's rise to power, by which the chief hotel of the place was momentarily graced. It had had as many official

25

names in its time as the square in which it stood—
the Royal, the Reform, the October Revolution,
the Empire, the President Coolidge, the Duchess of
Windsor—according to the humours of local history,
but Neutralians invariably spoke of it quite simply
as the ' Ritz.' It rose amid sub-tropical vegetation, fountains and statuary, a solid structure, orna-
mented in the rococo style of fifty years ago. Neutralians of the upper class congregated there,
sauntered about its ample corridors, sat in its comfortable foyer, used the concierge as a poste restante,
borrowed small sums from its barmen, telephoned
sometimes, gossiped always, now and then lightly
dozed. They did not spend any money there.
They could not afford to. The prices were fixed,
and fixed high, by law ; to them were added a
series of baffling taxes—30 per cent. for service,
2 per cent. for stamp duty, 30 per cent. for luxury
tax, 5 per cent. for the winter relief fund, 12 per
cent. for those mutilated in the revolution, 4 per
cent. municipal dues, 2 per cent. federal tax, 8 per
cent. for living accommodation in excess of minimum
requirements, and others of the same kind ; they
mounted up, they put the bedroom floors and the
brilliant dining-rooms beyond the reach of all but
foreigners.

There had been few in recent years ; official

hospitality alone flourished at the Ritz ; but still the sombre circle of Neutralian male aristocracy— for, in spite of numberless revolutions and the gross dissemination of free-thought, Neutralian ladies still modestly kept the house—foregathered there ; it was their club. They wore very dark suits and very stiff collars, black ties, black buttoned boots ; they smoked their cigarettes in long tortoiseshell holders ; their faces were brown and wizened ; they spoke of money and women, dryly and distantly, for they had never enough of either.

On this afternoon of summer when the traditional Bellacita season was in its last week and they were all preparing to remove to the seaside or to their family estates, about twenty of these descendants of the crusaders sat in the cool of the Ritz lounge. They were rewarded first by the spectacle of the foreign professors' arrival from the Ministry of Rest and Culture. Already they seemed hot and weary ; they had come to fetch their academic dress for the reception at the University. The last-comers—Scott-King, Whitemaid, Miss Sveningen and Miss Bombaum—had lost their luggage. Dr. Arturo Fe was like a flame at the reception desk ; he pleaded, he threatened, he telephoned. Some said the luggage was impounded at the customs, others that the taxi driver had stolen it. Presently it was discovered in a service lift abandoned on the top storey.

At last Dr. Fe assembled his scholars, Scott-King in his M.A. gown and hood, Whitemaid, more flamboyantly, in the robes of his new doctorate of Upsala. Among the vestments of many seats of learning, some reminiscent of Daumier's law courts, some of Mr. Will Hay of the music-hall stage, Miss Sveningen stood conspicuous in sports dress of zephyr and white shorts. Miss Bombaum refused to go. She had a story to file, she said.

The party trailed out through the swing doors into the dusty evening heat, leaving the noblemen to compare their impressions of Miss Sveningen's legs. The subject was not exhausted when they returned ; indeed, had it arisen earlier in the year it would have served as staple conversation for the whole Bellacita season.

The visit to the University had been severe, an hour of speeches followed by a detailed survey of the archives. 'Miss Sveningen, gentlemen,' said Dr. Fe. 'We are a little behind. The Municipality is already awaiting us. I shall telephone them that we are delayed. Do not put yourselves out.'

The party dispersed to their rooms and re-assembled in due time dressed in varying degrees of elegance. Dr. Fe was splendid, tight white waistcoat, onyx buttons, a gardenia, half a dozen miniature medals, a kind of sash. Scott-King and Whitemaid seemed definitely seedy beside him. But the little brown marquesses and counts had no eye for these things. They were waiting for Miss Sveningen. If her academic dress had exposed such uncovenanted mercies, such superb, such unpredictable expanses and lengths of flesh, what would she not show them when gowned for the evening ?

She came.

Chocolate - coloured silk enveloped her from collar-bone to humerus and hung to within a foot of the ground ; low-heeled black satin shoes covered feet which seemed now unusually large. She had bound a tartan fillet in her hair. She wore a broad patent-leather belt. She had a handkerchief artfully attached to her wrist by her watch-strap. For perhaps a minute the inky, simian eyes regarded her aghast ; then, one by one, with the languor born of centuries of hereditary disillusionment, the Knights of Malta rose from their places and sauntered with many nods to the bowing footmen towards the swing doors, towards the breathless square, towards the subdivided palaces where their wives awaited them.

'Come, lady and gentlemen,' said Dr. Arturo
Fe. 'The cars are here. We are eagerly expected
at the Hôtel-de-Ville.'

No paunch, no jowl, no ponderous dignity of the
counting-house or of civic office, no hint indeed of
pomp or affluence, marked the Lord Mayor of Bellacita. He was young, lean and plainly ill at ease ;
he was much scarred by his revolutionary exploits,
wore a patch on one eye and supported himself on
a crutch-stick. 'His Excellency, alas, does not
speak English,' said Dr. Fe as he presented Scott-
King and Whitemaid.

They shook hands. The Lord Mayor scowled and
muttered something in Dr. Fe's ear.

'His Excellency says it is a great pleasure to
welcome such illustrious guests. In the phrase of
our people he says his house is yours.'

The English stood aside and separated. Whitemaid had sighted a buffet at the far end of the
tapestried hall. Scott-King stood diffidently alone ;
a footman brought him a glass of sweet effervescent
wine. Dr. Fe brought him someone to talk to.

'Allow me to present Engineer Garcia. He is
an ardent lover of England.'

'Engineer Garcia,' said the newcomer.

'Scott-King,' said Scott-King.

' I have work seven years with the firm Green, Gorridge and Wright Limited at Salford. You know them well, no doubt ? '

' I am afraid not.'

' They are a very well-known firm, I think. Do you go often to Salford ? '

' I'm afraid I've never been there.'

' It is a very well-known town. What, please, is your town ? '

' I suppose, Granchester.'

' I am not knowing Granchester. It is a bigger town than Salford ? '

' No, much smaller.'

' Ah. In Salford is much industry.'

' So I believe.'

' How do you find our Neutralian champagne ? '

' Excellent.'

' It is sweet, eh ? That is because of our Neutralian sun. You prefer it to the champagne of France ? '

' Well, it is quite different, isn't it ? '

' I see you are a connoisseur. In France is no sun. Do you know the Duke of Westminster ? '

' No.'

' I saw him once at Biarritz. A fine man. A man of great propriety.'

' Indeed ? '

'Indeed. London is his propriety. Have you a propriety?'

'No.'

'My mother had a propriety but it is lost.'

The clamour in the hall was tremendous. Scott-King found himself the centre of an English-speaking group. Fresh faces, new voices crowded in on him. His glass was repeatedly filled; it was over-filled and boiled and cascaded on his cuff. Dr. Fe passed and re-passed. 'Ah, you have soon made friends.' He brought reinforcements; he brought more wine. 'This is a special bottle,' he whispered. 'Special for you, Professor,' and refilled Scott-King's glass with the same sugary froth as before. The din swelled. The tapestried walls, the painted ceiling, the chandeliers, the gilded architrave, danced and dazzled before his eyes.

Scott-King became conscious that Engineer Garcia was seeking to draw him into a more confidential quarter.

'How do you find our country, Professor?'

'Very pleasant, I assure you.'

'Not how you expected it, eh? Your papers do not say it is pleasant. How is it allowed to scandalise our country? Your papers tell many lies about us.'

'They tell lies about everyone, you know.'

32

'Please?'

'They tell lies about everyone,' shouted Scott-King.

'Yes, lies. You see for yourself it is perfectly quiet.'

'Perfectly quiet.'

'How, please?'

'Quiet,' yelled Scott-King.

'You find it too quiet? It will become more gay soon. You are a writer?'

'No, merely a poor scholar.'

'How, poor? In England you are rich, no? Here we must work very hard for we are a poor country. In Neutralia for a scholar of the first class the salary is 500 ducats a month. The rent of his apartment is perhaps 450 ducats. His taxes are 100. Oil is 30 ducats a litre. Meat is 45 ducats a kilo. So you see, we work.

'Dr. Fe is a scholar. He is also a lawyer, a judge of the Lower Court. He edits the *Historical Review*. He has a high position in the Ministry of Rest and Culture, also at the Foreign Office and the Bureau of Enlightenment and Tourism. He speaks often on the radio about the international situation. He owns one-third share in the Sporting Club. In all the New Neutralia I do not think there is anyone works harder than Dr. Fe, yet he is not rich as Mr.

33

Green, Mr. Gorridge and Mr. Wright were rich in Salford. And they scarcely worked at all. There are injustices in the world, Professor.'

'I think we must be quiet. The Lord Mayor wishes to make a speech.'

'He is a man of no cultivation. A politician. They say his mother . . .'

'Hush.'

'This speech will not be interesting, I believe.'

Something like silence fell on the central part of the hall. The Lord Mayor had his speech ready typed on a sheaf of papers. He squinnied at it with his single eye and began haltingly to read.

Scott-King slipped away. As though at a great distance he descried Whitemaid, alone at the buffet, and unsteadily made his way towards him.

'Are you drunk?' whispered Whitemaid.

'I don't think so—just giddy. Exhaustion and the noise.'

'I am drunk.'

'Yes. I can see you are.'

'How drunk would you say I was?'

'Just drunk.'

'My dear, my dear Scott-King, there if I may say so, you are wrong. In every degree and by every known standard I am very, very much more drunk than you give me credit for.'

'Very well. But let's not make a noise while the Mayor's speaking.'

'I do not profess to know very much Neutralian but it strikes me that the Mayor, as you call him, is talking the most consummate rot. What is more, I doubt very much that he is a mayor. Looks to me like a gangster.'

'Merely a politician, I believe.'

'That is worse.'

'The essential, the immediate need is somewhere to sit down.'

Though they were friends only of a day, Scott-King loved this man; they had suffered, were suffering, together; they spoke, pre-eminently, the same language; they were comrades in arms. He took Whitemaid by the arm and led him out of the hall to a cool and secluded landing where stood a little settee of gilt and plush, a thing not made for sitting on. Here they sat, the two dim men, while very faintly from behind them came the sound of oratory and applause.

'They were putting it in their pockets,' said Whitemaid.

'Who? What?'

'The servants. The food. In the pockets of those long braided coats they wear. They were taking it away for their families. I got four

35

macaroons.' And then swiftly veering he remarked : ' She looks terrible.'

' Miss Sveningen ? '

' That glorious creature. It was a terrible shock
to see her when she came down changed for the
party. It killed something here,' he said, touching
his heart.

' Don't cry.'

' I can't help crying. You've seen her brown
dress ? And the hair ribbon ? And the handkerchief ? '

' Yes, yes, I saw it all. And the belt.'

' The belt,' said Whitemaid, ' was more than
flesh and blood could bear. Something snapped,
here,' he said, touching his forehead. ' You must
remember how she looked in shorts ? A Valkyrie.
Something from the heroic age. Like some god-
like, some unimaginably strict school prefect, *a
dormitory monitor*,' he said in a kind of ecstasy.
' Think of her striding between the beds, a pigtail,
bare feet, in her hand a threatening hairbrush.
Oh, Scott-King, do you think she rides a bicycle ? '

' I'm sure of it.'

' In shorts ? '

' Certainly in shorts.'

' I can imagine a whole life lived riding tandem
behind her, through endless forests of conifers, and

at midday sitting down among the pine needles to eat hard-boiled eggs. Think of those strong fingers peeling an egg, Scott-King, the brown of it, the white of it, the shine. Think of her *biting* it.'

'Yes, it would be a splendid spectacle.'

'And then think of her now, in there, in that brown dress.'

'There are things not to be thought of, White-maid.' And Scott-King, too, shed a few tears of sympathy, of common sorrow in the ineffable, the cosmic sadness of Miss Sveningen's party frock.

'What is this?' said Dr. Fe, joining them some minutes later. 'Tears? You are not enjoying it?'

'It is only,' said Scott-King, 'Miss Sveningen's dress.'

'This is tragic, yes. But in Neutralia we take such things bravely, with a laugh. I came, not to intrude, simply to ask, Professor, you have your little speech ready for this evening? We count on you at the banquet to say a few words.'

For the banquet they returned to the Ritz. The foyer was empty save for Miss Bombaum who sat smoking a cigar with a man of repellent aspect. 'I have had my dinner. I'm going out after a story,' she explained.

It was half-past ten when they sat down at a

37

table spread with arabesques of flower-heads, petals, moss, trailing racemes and sprays of foliage until it resembled a parterre by Le Nôtre. Scott-King counted six wineglasses of various shapes standing before him amid the vegetation. A menu of enormous length, printed in gold, lay on his plate beside a typewritten place-card ' *Dr. Scotch-Kink.*' Like many explorers before him, he found that prolonged absence from food destroyed the appetite. The waiters had already devoured the *hors-d'œuvre*, but when at length the soup arrived, the first mouthful made him hiccup. This, too, he remembered, had befallen Captain Scott's doomed party in the Antarctic.

' Comment dit-on en français '' hiccup '' ? ' he asked his neighbour.

' Plaît-il, mon professeur ? '

Scott-King hiccuped. ' Ça,' he said.

' Ça c'est le hoquet.'

' J'en ai affreusement.'

' Évidemment, mon professeur. Il faut du cognac.'

The waiters had drunk and were drinking profusely of brandy and there was a bottle at hand. Scott-King tossed off a glassful and his affliction was doubled. He hiccuped without intermission throughout the long dinner.

38

This neighbour, who had so ill-advised him, was, Scott-King saw from the card, Dr. Bogdan Antonic, the International Secretary of the Association, a middle-aged, gentle man whose face was lined with settled distress and weariness. They conversed, as far as the hiccups permitted, in French.

'You are not Neutralian?'

'Not yet. I hope to be. Every week I make my application to the Foreign Office and always I am told it will be next week. It is not so much for myself I am anxious—though death is a fearful thing—as for my family. I have seven children, all born in Neutralia, all without nationality. If we are sent back to my unhappy country they would hang us all without doubt.'

'Jugo-Slavia?'

'I am a Croat, born under the Habsburg Empire. That was a true League of Nations. As a young man I studied in Zagreb, Budapest, Prague, Vienna—one was free, one moved where one would; one was a citizen of Europe. Then we were liberated and put under the Serbs. Now we are liberated again and put under the Russians. And always more police, more prisons, more hanging. My poor wife is Czech. Her nervous constitution is quite deranged by our troubles. She thinks all the time she is being watched.'

39

Scott-King essayed one of those little, inarticulate, non-committal grunts of sympathy which come easily to the embarrassed Englishman ; to an Englishman, that is, who is not troubled by the hiccups. The sound which in the event issued from him might have been taken as derisive by a less sensitive man than Dr. Antonic.

'I think so, too,' he said severely. 'There are spies everywhere. You saw that man, as we came in, sitting with the woman with the cigar. He is one of them. I have been here ten years and know them all. I was second secretary to our Legation. It was a great thing, you must believe, for a Croat to enter our diplomatic service. All the appointments went to Serbs. Now there is no Legation. My salary has not been paid since 1940. I have a few friends at the Foreign Office. They are sometimes kind and give me employment, as at the present occasion. But at any moment they may make a trade agreement with the Russians and hand us over.'

Scott-King attempted to reply.

'You must take some more brandy, Professor. It is the only thing. Often, I remember, in Ragusa I have had the hiccups from laughing. . . . Never again, I suppose.'

Though the company was smaller at the banquet

than at the *vin d'honneur*, the noise was more oppressive. The private dining-room of the Ritz, spacious as it was, had been built in a more trumpery style than the Hôtel-de-Ville. There the lofty roof had seemed to draw the discordant voices upwards into the cerulean perspective with which it was painted, and disperse them there amid the floating deities ; the Flemish hunting scenes on the walls seemed to envelop and muffle them in their million stitches. But here the din banged back from gilding and mirrors ; above the clatter and chatter of the dinner-table and the altercations of the waiters, a mixed choir of young people sang folk-songs, calculated to depress the most jovial village festival. It was not thus, in his class-room at Granchester, that Scott-King had imagined himself dining.

' At my little house on the point at Lapad, we used to sit on the terrace laughing so loudly, sometimes, that the passing fishermen called up to us from their decks asking to share the joke. They sailed close in-shore and one could follow their lights far out towards the islands. When we were silent, *their* laughter came to us across the water when they were out of sight.'

The neighbour on Scott-King's left did not speak until the dessert, except to the waiters ; to them he spoke loudly and often, sometimes blustering, sometimes cajoling, and by this means got two helpings of nearly every course. His napkin was tucked into his collar. He ate intently with his head bowed over his plate so that the morsels which frequently fell from his lips were not permanently lost to him. He swigged his wine with relish, sighing after each draught and tapping the glass with his knife to call the waiter's attention to the need of refilling it. Often he jammed glasses on his nose and studied the menu, not so much, it seemed, for fear of missing anything, as to fix in his memory the fleeting delights of the moment. It is not entirely easy to achieve a Bohemian appearance in evening-dress but this man did so with his shock of grizzled hair, the broad ribbon of his pince-nez, and a three days' growth of beard and whisker.

With the arrival of the dessert, he raised his countenance, fixed on Scott-King his large and rather bloodshot eyes, belched mildly and then spoke. The words were English; the accent had been formed in many cities from Memphis (Mo.) to Smyrna. 'Shakespeare, Dickens, Byron, Galsworthy,' he seemed to say.

This late birth of a troublesome gestation took Scott-King by surprise; he hiccuped non-committally.

'They are all great English writers.'

42

'Well, yes.'

'Your favourite, please?'

'I suppose Shakespeare.'

'He is the more dramatic, the more poetic, no?'

'Yes.'

'But Galsworthy is the more modern.'

'Very true.'

'I am modern. You are a poet?'

'Hardly that. A few translations.'

'I am an original poet. I translate my poems myself into English prose. They have been published in the United States. Do you read the *New Destiny*?'

'I am afraid not.'

'It is the magazine which publishes my translations. Last year they sent me ten dollars.'

'No one has ever paid me for my translations.'

'You should send them to the *New Destiny*. It is not possible, I think,' continued the Poet, 'to render the poetry of one language into the poetry of another. Sometimes I translate English prose into Neutralian poetry. I have done a very beautiful rendering of some selected passages of your great Priestley. I hoped it would be used in the High Schools but it is not. There is jealousy and intrigue everywhere—even at the Ministry of Education.'

At this moment a splendid figure at the centre of the table rose to make the first speech. 'Now to work,' said his neighbour, produced a note-book and pencil and began busily writing in shorthand. 'In the new Neutralia we all work.'

The speech was long and provoked much applause. In the course of it a note came to Scott-King by the hand of a waiter : '*I shall call on you to reply to his Excellency. Fe.*'

Scott-King wrote in answer : '*Terribly sorry. Not tonight. Indisposed. Ask Whitemaid,*' stealthily left his place and, still hiccuping, passed behind the table to the dining-room door.

Outside the foyer was almost deserted ; the great glass dome which throughout the years of war had blazed aloft nightly, a candle in a naughty world, rose darkly. Two night porters shared a cigar behind one of the pillars ; a huge empty carpet, strewn with empty chairs, lay before Scott-King in the subdued light to which a parsimonious management had reduced the earlier blaze. It was not much past midnight but in the New Neutralia memories persisted of the revolutionary curfew, of police round-ups, of firing squads in the public gardens ; New Neutralians liked to get home early and bolt their doors.

As Scott-King stepped into this silent space, his

hiccups mysteriously ceased. He went through the swing doors and breathed the air of the piazza where under the arc-lamps workmen were washing away with hoses the dust and refuse of the day ; the last of the trams, which all day long rattled round the fountains, had long since returned to its shed. He breathed deeply, testing, as it were, the limits of his miraculous recovery, and knew it to be complete. Then he turned back, took his key and, barely conscious, ascended.

During the first tumultuous afternoon and evening in Bellacita there had been little opportunity for more than the barest acquaintance between Scott-King and his fellow-guests of the Bellorius Association. Indeed he had scarcely distinguished them from their hosts. They had bowed and shaken hands, they had exchanged nods among the University archives, they had apologised one to the other as they jostled and jogged elbows at the *vin d'honneur* ; Scott-King had no share in whatever intimacies flourished after the banquet. He remembered an affable American and a Swiss of extreme hauteur and an oriental whom on general principles he assumed to be Chinese. Now on the morning following he came cheerfully to join them in the Ritz foyer in accordance with

45

the printed programme. They were to leave at 10.30 for Simona. His bags were packed ; the sun, not yet oppressive, shone brilliantly through the glass dome. He was in the best of tempers.

He had awoken in this rare mood after a night of untroubled sleep. He had breakfasted on a tray of fruit, sitting on his verandah above the square, showering copious blessings on the palms and fountains and trams and patriotic statuary. He approached the group in the foyer with the intention of making himself peculiarly agreeable.

Of the festive Neutralians of the day before only Dr. Fe and the Poet remained. The rest were at work elsewhere constructing the New Neutralia.

' Professor Scott-King, how are you this morning ? '

There was more than politeness in Dr. Fe's greeting ; there was definite solicitude.

' Extremely well, thank you. Oh, of course, I had forgotten about last night's speech. I was very sorry to fail you ; the truth was . . .'

' Professor Scott-King, say no more. Your friend Whitemaid I fear is not so well.'

' No ? '

' No. He has sent word that he cannot join us.' Dr. Fe raised exquisitely expressive eyebrows.

The Poet drew Scott-King momentarily aside.

46

'Do not be alarmed,' he said. 'Reassure your friend. Not a hint of last night's occurrences shall appear. I speak with the authority of the Ministry.'

'You know I'm completely in the dark.'

'So are the public. So they shall remain. You sometimes laugh at us in your democratic way for our little controls, but they have their uses, you see.'

'But I don't know what has happened.'

'So far as the press of Neutralia is concerned, nothing happened.'

The Poet had shaved that morning and shaved ruthlessly. The face he thrust near Scott-King's was tufted with cotton-wool. Now he withdrew it and edged away. Scott-King joined the group of delegates.

'Well,' said Miss Bombaum, 'I seemed to have missed a whole packet of fun last night.'

'I seem to have missed it too.'

'And how's the head this morning?' asked the American scholar.

'Seems like you had fun,' said Miss Bombaum.

'I went to bed early,' said Scott-King coldly. 'I was thoroughly over-tired.'

'Well, I've heard it called plenty of things in my time. I reckon that covers it too.'

Scott-King was an adult, an intellectual, a

classical scholar, almost a poet ; provident Nature who shields the slow tortoise and points the quills of the porcupine, has given to such tender spirits their appropriate armour. A shutter, an iron curtain, fell between Scott-King and these two jokers. He turned to the rest of the company and realised too late that jocularity was the least he had to fear. The Swiss had not been cordial the day before ; this morning he was theatrical in his coldness ; the Asiatic seemed to have spun himself a cocoon of silken aloofness. The assembled scholars did not positively cut Scott-King ; in their several national fashions they signified that they were not unaware of Scott-King's presence amongst them. Further than this they did not go. They too had their shutters, their iron curtains. Scott-King was in disgrace. Something unmentionable had happened in which he was vicariously but inextricably implicated ; a gross, black, inexpungible blot had fallen on Scott-King overnight.

He did not wish to know more. He was an adult, an intellectual ; he was all that has already been predicated of him. He was no chauvinist. Throughout six embattled years he had remained resolutely impartial. But now his hackles rose ; quite literally he felt the roots of his sparse hairs prick and tingle. Like the immortal private of the

Buffs he stood in Elgin's place ; not untaught certainly, nor rude, nor abysmally low-born, but poor and, at the moment, reckless, bewildered and alone, a heart with English instinct fraught he yet could call his own.

'I may have to keep the party waiting a few minutes,' he said. 'I must go and call on my colleague Mr. Whitemaid.'

He found him in bed looking strange rather than ill ; almost exalted. He was still rather drunk. The windows stood wide open on to the balcony and on the balcony, modestly robed in bath towels, sat Miss Sveningen eating beefsteak.

'They tell me downstairs that you are not coming with us to Simona ? '

'No. I'm not quite up to it this morning. I have things to attend to here. It is not easy for me to explain.' He nodded towards the giant carnivore on the balcony.

'You spent an agreeable evening ? '

'A total blank, Scott-King. I remember being with you at some kind of civic reception. I remember a fracas with the police, but that was much later. Hours must have intervened.'

'The police ? '

'Yes. At some kind of dancing place. Irma here was splendid—like something in a film.

49

They went down like nine-pins. But for her I suppose I should be in a cell at this moment instead of happily consuming bromoseltzer in your company.'

' You made a speech.'

' So I gather. You missed it? Then we shall never know what I said. Irma in her blunt way described it as long and impassioned but incomprehensible.'

' Was it about Bellorius?'

' I rather suppose not. Love was uppermost in my mind, I think. To tell you the truth I have lost my interest in Bellorius. It was never strong. It wilted and died this morning when I learned that Irma was not of us. She has come for the Physical Training Congress.'

' I shall miss you.'

' Stay with us for the gymnastics.'

For a second Scott-King hesitated. The future at Simona was obscure and rather threatening.

' There are to be five hundred female athletes. Contortionists perhaps from the Indies.'

' No,' said Scott-King at length firmly. ' I must keep faith with Bellorius.'

And he returned to the delegates who now sat impatiently in a charabanc at the doors of the Ritz.

THE town of Simona stands within sight of the Mediterranean Sea on the foothills of the great massif which fills half the map of Neutralia. Groves of walnut and cork-oak, little orchards of almond and lemon, cover the surrounding country and grow to the foot of the walls which jut out among them in a series of sharp bastions, ingeniously contrived in the seventeenth century and never, in a long history of strife, put to the test of assault ; for they enclose

51

little of military significance. The medieval university, the baroque cathedral, twenty churches in whose delicate limestone belfries the storks build and multiply, a rococo square, two or three tiny shabby palaces, a market and a street of shops are all that can be found there and all that the heart of man can properly desire. The railway runs well clear of the town and betrays its presence only by rare puffs of white smoke among the tree-tops.

At the hour of the angelus Scott-King sat with Mr. Bogdan Antonic at a café table on the ramparts.

' I suppose Bellorius must have looked out on almost precisely the same prospect as we see today.'

' Yes, the buildings at least do not change. There is still the illusion of peace while, as in Bellorius's time, the hills behind us are a nest of brigands.'

' He alludes to them, I remember, in the eighth canto, but surely today ? . . .'

' It is still the same. Now they call them by different names—partisans, resistance groups, unreconcilables, what you will. The effect is the same. You need police escort to travel many of the roads.'

They fell silent. In the course of the circuitous journey to Simona, sympathy had sprung up

52

between Scott-King and the International Secretary.

Bells deliciously chimed in the sunlit towers of twenty shadowy churches.

At length Scott-King said : ' You know I suspect that you and I are the only members of our party who have read Bellorius.'

' My own knowledge of him is slight. But Mr. Fu has written of him very feelingly, I believe, in demotic Cantonese. Tell me, Professor, do you think the celebration is a success ? '

' I'm not really a professor, you know.'

' No, but for the occasion all are professors. You are more professor than some who are here. I was obliged to cast my net rather wide to have all countries represented. Mr. Jungman, for example, is simply a gynaecologist from the Hague, and Miss Bombaum is I do not know what. The Argentine and the Peruvian are mere students who happened to be in the country at this time. I tell you these things because I trust you and because I think you suspect them already. You have not perceived an element of deception ? '

' Well, yes.'

' It is the wish of the Ministry. You see, I am their cultural adviser. They required a celebration this summer. I searched the records for an anniversary. I was in despair until by chance I hit on the name of Bellorius. They had not heard of him, of course, but then they would have been equally in the dark if he had been Dante or Goethe. I told them,' said Mr. Antonic with a sad, sly, highly civilised little smile, ' that he was one of the greatest figures of European letters.'

' So he should be.'

' You really think so ? You do not find the whole thing a masquerade ? You think it is a success ? I hope so, for you see my position at the Ministry is far from secure. There is jealousy everywhere. Imagine it, that anyone should be jealous of *me*. But in the New Neutralia all are so eager to work. They would snap up my little post greedily. Dr. Arturo Fe would like it.'

' Surely not ? He seems fully employed already.'

' That man collects government posts as in the old days churchmen collected benefices. He has a dozen already and he covets mine. That is why it is such a triumph to have brought him here. If the celebration is not a success, he will be implicated. Already, today, the Ministry have shown displeasure that the statue of Bellorius is not ready to be unveiled tomorrow. It is not our fault. It is the Office of Rest and Culture. It is the plot of an enemy named Engineer Garcia, who seeks to ruin Dr. Fe and to succeed him in some of his posts.

54

But Dr. Fe will explain ; he will improvise.   He is of the country.'

Dr. Fe improvised next day.

The party of savants were quartered in the main hotel of Simona, which that morning had the aspect of a war-time railway station owing to the arrival some time after midnight of fifty or sixty international philatelists for whom no accommodation had been arranged.   They had slept in the lounge and hall ; were, some of them, still sleeping when the Bellorius delegation assembled.

This was the day set down in the programme for the unveiling of the Bellorius statue.   Hoarding and scaffolding in the town square marked the site of the proposed monument, but it was already well known among the delegates that the statue had not arrived.   They had lived by rumour during the past three days for nothing in their exhilarating experiences had quite corresponded with the printed plan.   ' They say the bus has gone back to Bella-cita for new tyres.'—' Have you heard we are to dine with the Lord Mayor ? '—' I heard Dr. Fe say we should not leave till three o'clock.'—' I believe we ought all to be at the Chapter House ' . . . and so on.   This was the atmosphere of the tour, and in it the social barriers which had threatened to divide them at Bellacita had quickly broken down. Whitemaid was forgotten, Scott-King found himself once more befriended, made part of a fellowship of bewilderment. They were two days on the road sleeping at places far from their original route ; they were wined and feasted at unexpected hours, disconcertingly greeted by brass bands and deputations, disconcertingly left stranded in deserted squares ; once they crossed paths and for several frantic hours exchanged luggage with a party of religious pilgrims ; once they had two dinners within an hour of each other ; once they had none. But here they were in the end where they should be, at Simona. The only absentee was Bellorius.

Dr. Fe improvised.

'Miss Bombaum, gentlemen, a little addition to our programme. Today we go to pay homage to the National Memorial.' Obediently they trooped out to the bus. Some philatelists were sleeping there and had to be dislodged. With them were embarked a dozen vast wreaths of laurel.

'What are these ? '

'Those are our homage.'

Red ribbons across the foliage bore the names of the countries thus curiously represented.

They drove out of the town into the land of

56

cork-oak and almond. After an hour they were stopped and an escort of armoured cars formed up before and behind them.

'A little token of our esteem," said Dr. Fe.

'It is for fear of the partisans,' whispered Dr. Antonic.

Dust from the military enveloped the bus and hid the landscape. After two hours they halted. Here on a bare hillock stood the National Memorial. Like all modern state-architecture it was a loveless, unadorned object saved from insignificance only by its bulk ; a great truncated pyramid of stone. A squad of soldiers were at work seeking lethargic-ally to expunge a message daubed across the inscribed face in red paint : ' Death to the Marshal.'

Dr. Fe ignored their activities and led his party to the further side which was innocent of any legend, patriotic or subversive. Here under a fierce sun they left their wreaths, Scott-King stepping forward, when called, to represent Great Britain. The poet-journalist crouched and snapped with his camera. The escort cheered. The fatigue-men came round with their mops to see what was going on. Dr. Fe said a few words in Neutralian. The ceremony was over. They had luncheon in a neighbouring town at what seemed to be a kind of barrack-canteen, a bare room decorated only by a large photograph of the Marshal ; a substantial but far from sumptuous meal eaten at narrow tables on thick earthenware plates. Scott-King drank several glasses of the heavy, purplish wine. The bus had stood long in the sun and was scorching hot. The wine and the thick stew induced sleep, and Scott-King lolled away the hours of the return journey unconscious of the jungle-whispering which prevailed around him in that tropic air.

Whispering, however, there was, and it found full voice when at length the party returned to Simona.

Scott-King awoke to it as he entered the hotel. ' We must call a meeting,' the American professor was saying. ' We must vote a resolution.'

' We want a show-down,' said Miss Bombaum. ' Not here,' she added, taking stock of the stamp-collectors who still squatted in the public rooms. ' Upstairs.'

It would be tedious in the extreme to recount all that was said in Miss Bombaum's bedroom after the expulsion of two philatelists who had taken refuge there. It was tedious to sit there, thought Scott-King, while the fountains were splashing in the square and the breeze stirring among the orange leaves on the city walls. Speeches were made,

58

repeated, translated and mis-translated ; there were calls for order and small private explosions of ill-temper. Not all the delegates were present. The Swiss Professor and the Chinese could not be found ; the Peruvian and Argentine students refused to come, but there were six savants in the little bed-room besides Miss Bombaum, all of them, except Scott-King, very indignant about something.

The cause of offence emerged through many words and the haze of tobacco smoke. In brief it was this : the Bellorius Association had been made dupes of the politicians. But for Miss Bombaum's insatiable curiosity nothing need ever have been known of it. She had nosed out the grim truth like a truffle and the fact was plain. The National Monument was nothing more or less than a fetish of civil strife. It commemorated the massacre, execu-tion, liquidation—what you will—ten years back on that sunny spot of some fifty leaders of the now domi-nant Neutralian party by those then dominant. The delegates of the Bellorius Association had been tricked into leaving wreaths there and, worse than this, had been photographed in the act. Miss Bom-baum's picture was at that moment, she said, being rushed out to the newspapers of the world. More than this they had lunched at the party Head-quarters at the very tables where the ruffians of the party were wont to refresh themselves after their orgies of terrorisation. What was more, Miss Bombaum said, she had just learned from a book in her possession that Bellorius had never had any connection with Neutralia at all; he had been a Byzantine general.

Scott-King petulantly joined issue on this point. Strong words were used of him. 'Fascist beast.'—'Reactionary cannibal.'—'Bourgeois escapist.'

Scott-King withdrew from the meeting.

Dr. Fe was in the passage. He took Scott-King's arm and silently led him downstairs and out into the arcaded street.

'They are not content,' said Dr. Fe. 'It is a tragedy of the first magnitude.'

'You shouldn't have done it, you know,' said Scott-King.

'*I* should not have done it? My dear Professor, I wept when it was first suggested. I delayed our journey two days on the road precisely to avoid this. But would they listen? I said to the Minister of Popular Enlightenment: "Excellency, this is an international occasion. It is in the realm of pure scholarship. These great men have not come to Neutralia for political purposes." He replied coarsely: "They are eating and drinking at our expense. They should show their respect for the

60

Régime. The Physical Training delegates have all saluted the Marshal in the Sports Stadium. The philatelists have been issued with the party badge and many of them wear it. The professors, too, must help the New Neutralia." What could I say? He is a person of no delicacy, of the lowest origins. It was he, I have no doubt, who induced the Ministry of Rest and Culture to delay sending the statue. Professor, you do not understand politics. I will be frank with you. It was all a plot.'

' So Miss Bombaum says.'

' A plot against me. For a long time now they have been plotting my downfall. I am not a party man. You think because I wear the badge and give the salute I am of the New Neutralia. Professor, I have six children, two of them girls of marriageable age. What can one do but seek one's fortune? And now I think I am ruined.'

' Is it as bad as that?'

' I cannot express how bad it is. Professor, you must go back to that room and persuade them to be calm. You are English. You have great influence. I have remarked during our journey together how they have all respected you.'

' They called me " a fascist beast." '

' Yes,' said Dr. Fe simply, ' I heard it through the keyhole. They were very discontented.'

After Miss Bombaum's bedroom, the streets were cool and sweet ; the touch of Dr. Fe's fingers on Scott-King's sleeve was light as a moth. They walked on in silence. At a dewy flower-stall Dr. Fe chose a buttonhole, haggled fiercely over the price, presented it with Arcadian grace to Scott-King and then resumed the sorrowful promenade.

' You will not go back ? '

' It would do no good, you know.'

' An Englishman admits himself beaten,' said Dr. Fe desperately.

' It amounts to that.'

' But you yourself will stay with us to the end ? '

' Oh certainly.'

' Why, then, we have lost nothing of consequence. The celebrations can proceed.' He said it politely, gallantly, but he sighed as they parted.

Scott-King climbed the worn steps of the ramparts and sat alone under the orange trees watching the sun set.

The hotel was tranquil that evening. The philatelists had been collected and carted off ; they left dumbly and glumly for an unknown destination like Displaced Persons swept up in the machinery of ' social engineering.' The six dissident delegates went with them, in default of other transport. The Swiss, the Chinese, the Peruvian and the Argentine alone remained. They dined together, silently, lacking a common tongue, but in good humour. Dr. Fe, Dr. Antonic and the Poet dined at another table, also silent, but sorrowful.

Next day the errant effigy arrived by lorry and the day following was fixed for the unveiling. Scott-King passed the time happily. He studied the daily papers, all of which, true to Miss Bombaum's forecast, displayed large photographs of the ceremony at the National Monument. He pieced together the sense of a leading article on the subject, he ate, he dozed, he visited the cool and glowing churches of the town, he composed the speech which, he was told, was expected of him on the morrow. Dr. Fe, when they met, showed the reserve proper to a man of delicate feeling who had in emotion revealed too much of himself. It was a happy day for Scott-King.

Not so for his colleagues. Two disasters befell them severally, while he was pottering around. The Swiss Professor and the Chinese went for a little drive together in the hills. Their companionship was grounded on economy rather than mutual liking. An importunate guide ; insensibility to the contemplative pleasures of Western architecture ; a seemingly advantageous price ; the promise of cool breezes, a wide panorama, a little restaurant ; these undid them. When at evening they had not returned, their fate was certain.

'They should have consulted Dr. Fe,' said Dr. Antonic.

'He would have chosen a more suitable road and found them an escort.'

'What will become of them ? '

'With the partisans you cannot say. Many of them are worthy, old-fashioned fellows who will treat them hospitably and wait for a ransom. But some are occupied with politics. If our friends have fallen among those, I am afraid they will certainly be murdered.

'I did not like the Swiss.'

'Nor I. A Calvinist. But the Ministry will not be pleased that he is murdered.'

The fate of the South Americans was less romantic. The police took them off during luncheon.

'It seems they were not Argentine or Peruvian,' said Dr. Antonic. 'Not even students.'

'What had they done ? '

'I suppose they were informed against.'

'They certainly had a villainous appearance.'

'Oh yes, I suppose they were desperate fellows—spies, bimetallists, who can say ? Nowadays it is not what you do that counts, but who informs against you. I think someone very high up must have informed against that pair. Otherwise Dr. Fe could have had the business postponed until after our little ceremony. Or perhaps Dr. Fe's influence is on the wane.'

So in the end, as was indeed most fitting, one voice only was raised to honour Bellorius.

The statue, when at last after many ineffective tugs at the controlling cord, it was undraped and stood clear, stonily, insolently unabashed under the fierce Neutralian sun, while the populace huzzaed and, according to their custom, threw fire-crackers under the feet of the notables, as the pigeons fluttered above in high alarm and the full weight of the band followed the opening trumpets—the statue was appalling.

There are no contemporary portraits of Bellorius still extant. In their absence some sharp business had been done in the Ministry of Rest and Culture. The figure now so frankly brought to view had lain long years in a mason's yard. It had been commissioned in an age of free enterprise for the tomb of a commercial magnate whose estate, on his death, had proved to be illusory. It was not Bellorius ; it was not the fraudulent merchant prince ; it was not even unambiguously male ; it was scarcely human ; it represented perhaps one of the virtues.

Scott-King stood aghast at the outrage he had unwittingly committed on that gracious square. But he had already spoken and his speech had been a success. He had spoken in Latin ; he had spoken from the heart. He had said that a torn and embittered world was that day united in dedicating itself to the majestic concept of Bellorius, in rebuilding itself first in Neutralia, then among all the yearning peoples of the West, on the foundations Bellorius had so securely laid. He had said that they were lighting a candle that day which by the Grace of God should never be put out.

And after the oration came a prodigious luncheon at the University. And after the luncheon he was invested with a Doctorate of International Law. And after the investiture he was put into a bus and driven with Dr. Fe, Dr. Antonic and the Poet, back to Bellacita.

By the direct road the journey took barely five hours. It was not yet midnight when they drove down the brilliant boulevard of the capital city. Little had been said on the road. When they drew up at the Ministry, Dr. Fe said : ' So our little expedition is over. I can only hope, Professor, that you have enjoyed it a particle as much as we.' He held out his hand and smiled under the arc-lamps. Dr. Antonic and the Poet collected their modest luggage. 'Good night,' they said. 'Good night. We shall walk from here. The taxis are so expensive—the double fare operates after nine o'clock.'

They walked. Dr. Fe ascended the steps of the Ministry. 'Back to work,' he said. 'I have had an urgent summons to report to my chief. We work late in the New Neutralia.'

There was nothing furtive about his ascent but it was swift. Scott-King caught him as he was about to enter a lift.

'But, I say, where am I to go?'

'Professor, our humble town is yours. Where would you like to go?'

'Well, I suppose I must go to an hotel. We were at the Ritz before.'

'I am sure you will be comfortable there. Tell the porter to get you a taxi and see he does not try to overcharge you. Double fare but not more.'

'But I shall see you tomorrow?'

'I hope *very* often.'

Dr. Fe bowed and the doors of the lift shut upon his bow and his smile.

There was in his manner something more than the reserve proper to a man of delicate feeling who had in emotion revealed too much of himself.

67

'OFFICIALLY,' said Mr. Horace Smudge, ' we don't even know you're here.'

He gazed at Scott-King through hexagonal spectacles across the Pending Tray and twiddled a new-fangled fountain pen ; a multiplicity of pencils protruded from his breast-pocket and his face seemed to suggest that he expected one of the telephones on his desk to ring at any moment with a message about something far more important than the matter under discussion ; he was for all the world, Scott-King thought, like the clerk in the food office at Granchester.

Scott-King's life had been lived far from chanceries, but once, very many years ago at Stockholm, he had been asked to luncheon, by mistake for someone else, at the British Embassy. Sir Samson Courtenay had been *chargé d'affaires* at the time and Scott-King gratefully recalled the air of nonchalant benevolence with which he had received a callow undergraduate where he had expected a Cabinet Minister. Sir Samson had not gone far in his profession but for one man at least, for Scott-King, he remained the fixed type of English diplomat.

Smudge was not as Sir Samson ; he was the child of sterner circumstances and a more recent theory of public service ; no uncle had put in a bland word for Smudge in high places ; honest toil, a clear head in the examination room, a genuine enthusiasm for Commercial Geography, had brought him to his present position as second secretary at Bellacita. ' You've no conception,' said Smudge, ' what a time we have with Priorities. I've had to put the Ambassadress off the plane twice, at the last moment, to make room for I.C.I. men. As it is I have four electrical engineers, two British Council lecturers and a trades unionist all wanting passages. Officially we have not heard of Bellorius. The Neutralians brought you here. It's their business to get you back.'

'I've been to them twice a day for three days. The man who organised everything, Dr. Fe, seems to have left the Ministry.'

'You could always go by train, of course. It takes a little time but it would probably be quicker in the end. I presume you have all the necessary visas?'

'No. How long would they take to get?'

'Perhaps three weeks, perhaps longer. It's the Inter-Allied Zone Authority which holds things up.'

'But I can't afford to go on living here indefinitely. I was only allowed to bring £75 and the prices are terrible.'

'Yes, we had a case like that the other day. A man called Whitemaid. He'd run out of money and wanted to cash a cheque, but of course that is specifically contrary to the currency regulations. The consul took charge of him.'

'Did he get home?'

'I doubt it. They used to ship them by sea, you know, as Distressed British Subjects and hand them over to the police on arrival, but all that has been discontinued since the war. He was connected with your Bellorius celebration I think. It has caused a good deal of work to us one way and another. But it's worse for the Swiss. They've had a professor murdered and that always involves a special report on counsellor-level. I'm sorry I can't do more for you. I only deal with air priorities. You are the business of the consulate really. You had better let them know in a week or two how things turn out.'

The heat was scarcely endurable. In the ten days Scott-King had been in the country, the summer seemed to change temper and set its face angrily against him. The grass had turned brown in the square. Men still hosed the streets but the burning stone was dry again in an instant. The season was over ; half the shops were shut and the little brown noblemen had left their chairs in the Ritz.

It was no great distance from the Embassy to the hotel, but Scott-King was stumbling with exhaustion before he reached the revolving doors. He went on foot for he was obsessed now by parsimony ; he could no longer eat with pleasure, counting the price of each mouthful, calculating the charge for service, the stamp duty, the luxury taxes ; groaning in that scorching summer under the weight of the Winter Relief Fund. He should leave the Ritz without delay, he resolved, and yet he hesitated ; once ensconced in some modest pension, in some remote side street where no telephone ever rang and no one in passage from the outer world ever set foot, might he not be lost irretrievably, submerged, unrecognisable in his dimness, unremembered ? Would he perhaps, years hence, exhibit a little discoloured card advertising lessons in English conversation, grow shabbier and greyer and plumper with the limp accretions of despair and destitution and die there at last nameless ? He was an adult, an intellectual, a classical scholar, almost a poet, but he could not face that future without terror. So he clung to the Ritz, empty as it was, contemptuously as he felt himself regarded there, as the one place in Neutralia where salvation might still be found. If he left, he knew it would be for ever. He lacked the assurance of the native nobility who could sit there day by day, as though by right. Scott-King's only right lay in his travellers' cheques. He worked out his bill from hour to hour. At the moment he had nearly forty pounds in hand. When he was down to twenty, he decided, he would move. Meanwhile he looked anxiously round the dining-room before starting the daily calculation of how cheaply he could lunch.

And that day he was rewarded. His number turned up. Sitting not two tables away, alone, was Miss Bombaum. He rose to greet her. All the hard epithets with which they had parted were forgotten.

'May I sit here?'

She looked up, first without recognition, then with pleasure. Perhaps there was something in his forlorn appearance, in the diffidence of his appeal, which cleared him in Miss Bombaum's mind. This was no fascist beast that stood before her, no reactionary cannibal.

'Surely,' she said. 'The guy who invited me hasn't shown up.'

A ghastly fear, cold in that torrid room, struck Scott-King, that he would have to pay for Miss Bombaum's luncheon. She was eating a lobster, he noted, and drinking hock.

'When you've finished,' he said. 'Afterwards, with coffee perhaps in the lounge.'

'I've a date in twenty minutes,' she said. 'Sit down.'

He sat and at once, in answer to her casual enquiry, poured out the details of his predicament. He laid particular stress on his financial problems and, as pointedly as he could, ordered the humblest dish on the menu. 'It's a fallacy not to eat in hot

73

weather,' said Miss Bombaum. ' You need to keep your resistance up.'

When he had finished the recital she said, ' Well, I reckon it shouldn't be hard to fix you up. Go by the Underground.'

Blacker despair in Scott-King's haunted face told Miss Bombaum that she had not made herself clear.

' You've surely heard of the Underground ? It's—' she quoted from one of her recent articles on the subject—' it's an alternative map of Europe, like a tracing overlying all the established frontiers and routes of communication. It's the new world taking shape below the surface of the old. It's the new ultra-national citizenship.'

' Well I'm blessed.'

' Look, I can't stop now. Be here this evening and I'll take you to see the key man.'

That afternoon, his last, as it turned out, in Bellacita, Scott-King received his first caller. He had gone to his room to sleep through the heat of the day, when his telephone rang and a voice announced Dr. Antonic. He asked for him to be sent up.

The Croat entered and sat by his bed.

' So you have acquired the Neutralian custom of the *siesta*. I am too old. I cannot adapt myself to new customs. Everything in this country is as strange to me as when I first came here.

'I was at the Foreign Office this morning enquiring about my papers of naturalisation and I heard by chance you were still here. So I came at once. I do not intrude? I thought you would have left by now. You have heard of our misfortunes? Poor Dr. Fe is disgraced. All his offices taken from him. More than this there is trouble with his accounts. He spent more, it appears, on the Bellorius celebrations than the Treasury authorised. Since he is out of office he has no access to the books and cannot adjust them. They say he will be prosecuted, perhaps sent to the islands.'

'And you, Dr. Antonic?'

'I am never fortunate. I relied on Dr. Fe for my naturalisation. Whom shall I turn to now? My wife thought that perhaps you could do something for us in England to make us British subjects.'

'There is nothing I can do.'

'No, I suppose not. Nor in America?'

'Still less there.'

'So I told my wife. But she is a Czech and so more hopeful. We Croats do not hope. It would be a great honour if you would come and explain these things to her. She will not believe me when I say there is no hope. I promised I would bring you.'

So Scott-King dressed and was led through the

heat to a new quarter on the edge of the town, to a block of flats.

'We came here because of the elevator. My wife was weary of Neutralian stairs. But alas the elevator no longer works.'

They trudged to the top floor, to a single sitting-room full of children, heavy with the smell of coffee and cigarette smoke.

'I am ashamed to receive you in a house without an elevator,' said Mme. Antonic in French ; then turning to the children, she addressed them in another tongue. They bowed, curtsied, and left the room. Mme. Antonic prepared coffee and brought a plate of biscuits from the cupboard.

'I was sure you would come,' she said. 'My husband is too timid. You will take us with you to America.'

'Dear madam, I have never been there.'

'To England then. We must leave this country. We are not at our ease here.'

'I am finding the utmost difficulty in getting to England myself.'

'We are respectable people. My husband is a diplomat. My father had his own factory at Budweis. Do you know Mr. Mackenzie ?'

'No, I don't think so.'

'He was a *very* respectable Englishman. He

would explain that we come of good people. He visited often to my father's factory. If you will find Mr. Mackenzie he will help us.'

So the conversation wore on. 'If we could only find Mr. Mackenzie,' Mme. Antonic repeated, 'all our troubles would be at an end.' Presently the children returned.

'I will take them to the kitchen,' said Mme. Antonic, 'and give them some jam. Then they will not be a nuisance.'

'You see,' said Dr. Antonic, as the door closed, 'she is always hopeful. Now I do not hope. Do you think,' he asked, 'that in Neutralia Western Culture might be born again? That this country has been preserved by Destiny from the horrors of war so that it can become a beacon of hope for the world?'

'No,' said Scott-King.

'Do you not?' asked Dr. Antonic anxiously. 'Do you not? Neither do I.'

That evening Miss Bombaum and Scott-King took a cab to the suburbs and left it at a café where they met a man who had sat with Miss Bombaum in the Ritz on her first evening. No names were exchanged.

'Who's this guy, Martha?'

77

' An English friend of mine I want you to help.'

' Going far ? '

' England.   Can he see the chief ? '

' I go ask.   He's on the level ? '

' Surely.'

' Well, stick around while I ask.'

He went to telephone and returned saying, ' The chief'll see him.   We can drop him off there, then have our talk.'

They took another cab and drove further from the city into a district of tanneries and slaughter-houses, recognisable by their smell in the hot dark-ness.   Presently they stopped at a lightless villa.

' In there.   Don't ring.   Just push the door.'

' Hope you have a good trip,' said Miss Bom-baum.

Scott-King was not a reader of popular novels and so was unfamiliar with the phrase ' It all hap-pened so quickly that it was not until afterwards . . .'   That, however, expressed his situation. The cab drove off as he was still stumbling up the garden path.   He pushed the door, entered an empty and lightless hall, heard a voice from another room call ' Come in,' went in, and found himself in a shabby office confronting a Neutralian in the uniform of a major of police.

The man addressed him in English.   ' You are

Miss Bombaum's friend ? Sit down. Do not be alarmed by my uniform. Some of our clients are *very* much alarmed. A silly boy tried to shoot me last week when he saw me like this. He suspected a trap. You want to go to England, I think. That is very difficult. Now if you had said Mexico or Brazil or Switzerland it would be easier. You have reasons which make England preferable ? '

' I have reasons.'

' Curious. I spent many years there and found it a place of few attractions. The women had no modesty, the food upset my stomach. I have a little party on their way to Sicily. That would not do instead ? '

' I am afraid not.'

' Well, we must see what can be done. You have a passport ? This is lucky. English passports come very dear just now. I hope Miss Bombaum explained to you that mine is not a charitable organisation. We exist to make profits and our expenses are high. I am constantly bothered by people who come to me supposing I work for the love of it. I do love my work, but love is not enough. The young man I spoke of just now, who tried to shoot me—he is buried just outside under the wall—he thought this was a political organisation. We help people irrespective of class, race,

79

party, creed or colour—for cash in advance. It is true, when I first took over, there were certain amateur associations that had sprung up during the World War—escaping prisoners, communist agents, Zionists, spies and so on. I soon put them out of business. That is where my position in the police is a help. Now I can say I have a virtual monopoly. Our work increases every day. It is extraordinary how many people without the requisite facilities seem anxious to cross frontiers today. I also have a valued connection with the Neutralian government. Troublesome fellows whom they want to disappear pass through my hands in large numbers. How much have you got?'

'About forty pounds.'

'Show me.'

Scott-King handed him his book of travellers' cheques.

'But there are seventy pounds here.'

'Yes, but my hotel bill . . .'

'There will be no time for that.'

'I am sorry,' said Scott-King firmly. 'I could not possibly leave an hotel with my bill unpaid, especially in a foreign country. It may seem absurdly scrupulous to you but it is one of the things a Granchesterian simply cannot do.'

The Major was not a man to argue from first

principles. He took men as they came and in his humane calling he dealt with many types.

'Well, I shan't pay it,' he said. 'Do you know anyone else in Bellacita?'

'No one.'

'Think.'

'There was a man called Smudge at our Embassy.'

'Smudge shall have your bill. These cheques want signing.'

Despite his high training Scott-King signed and the cheques were put away in the bureau drawer.

'My luggage?'

'We do not handle luggage. You will start this evening. I have a small party leaving for the coast. We have our main clearing-house at Santa Maria. From there you will travel by steamer, perhaps not in the grand luxury, but what will you? No doubt as an Englishman you are a good sailor.'

He rang a bell on his desk and spoke to the answering secretary in rapid Neutralian.

'My man here will take charge of you and fit you out. You speak Neutralian? No? Perhaps it is as well. We do not encourage talk in my business, and I must warn you, the strictest discipline has to be observed. From now on you are

81

under orders. Those who disobey never reach their destinations. Goodbye and a good journey.'

Some few hours later a large and antiquated saloon car was bumping towards the sea. In it sat in extreme discomfort seven men habited as Ursuline nuns. Scott-King was among them.

The little Mediterranean seaport of Santa Maria lay very near the heart of Europe. An Athenian colony had thrived there in the days of Pericles and built a shrine to Poseidon ; Carthaginian slaves had built the breakwater and deepened the basin ; Romans had brought fresh water from the mountain springs ; Dominican friars had raised the great church which gave the place its present name ; the Habsburgs had laid out the elaborate little piazza ; one of Napoleon's marshals had made it his base and left a classical garden there. The footprints of all these gentler conquerors were still plain to see but Scott-King saw nothing as, at dawn, he bowled over the cobbles to the water-front.

The Underground dispersal centre was a warehouse ; three wide floors, unpartitioned, with boarded windows, joined by an iron staircase. There was one door near which the guardian had set her large brass bedstead. At most hours of the day she reclined there under a coverlet littered with various kinds of food, weapons, tobacco and a little bolster on which she sometimes made lace of an ecclesiastical pattern. She had the face of a *tricoteuse* of the Terror. 'Welcome to Modern Europe,' she said as the seven Ursulines entered.

The place was crowded. In the six days which he spent there Scott-King identified most of the groups who messed together by languages. There were a detachment of Slovene royalists, a few Algerian nationals, the remnants of a Syrian anarchist association, ten patient Turkish prostitutes, four French Pétainist millionaires, a few Bulgarian terrorists, a half-dozen former Gestapo men, an Italian air-marshal and his suite, a Hungarian ballet, some Portuguese Trotskyites. The English-speaking group consisted chiefly of armed deserters from the American and British Armies of Liberation. They had huge sums of money distributed about the linings of their clothes, the reward of many months' traffic round the docks of the central sea.

Such activity as there was took place in the hour before dawn. Then the officer in charge, husband, it seemed, of the guardian hag, would appear with lists and a handful of passports ; a roll would be called and a party despatched. During the day the soldiers played poker—a fifty-dollar ante and a hundred-dollar raise. Sometimes in the hours of darkness there were newcomers. The total number at the clearing station remained fairly constant.

At last on the sixth day there was a commotion. It began at midday with a call from the chief of police. He came with sword and epaulettes and he talked intently and crossly in Neutralian with the custodian.

One of the Americans, who had picked up more languages during his time in the Old World than most diplomats, explained : ' The guy with the fancy fixings says we got to get to hell out of here. Seems there's a new officer going to raid this joint.'

When the officer had gone, the custodian and his wife debated the question. ' The old girl says why don't he hand us over and get rewarded. The guy says Hell, the most likely reward they'd get would be hanging. Seems there's some stiffs planted round about.'

Presently a sea-captain appeared and talked Greek. All the Underground travellers sat stock still listening, picking up a word here and there. ' This guy's got a ship can take us off.'

' Where ? '

' Aw, some place. Seems they're kinda more interested in finance than geography.'

A bargain was struck. The captain departed,

and the Underground conductor explained to each
language group in turn that there had been a slight
dislocation of plan. ' Don't worry,' he said. ' Just
go quiet. Everything's all right. We'll look after
you. You'll all get where you want to in time.
Just at the moment you got to move quick and quiet,
that's all.'

So, unprotesting, at nightfall, the strangely
assorted party was hustled on board a schooner.
Noah's animals cannot have embarked with less
sense of the object of their journey. The little
ship was not built for such cargo. Down they went
into a dark hold ; hatches were battened down ;
the unmistakeable sound of moorings being cast off
came to them in their timbered prison ; an
auxiliary diesel engine started up ; sails were
hoisted ; soon they were on the high seas in very
nasty weather.

This is the story of a summer holiday ; a light
tale. It treats, at the worst, with solid discomfort
and intellectual doubt. It would be inappropriate
to speak here of those depths of the human spirit,
the agony and despair, of the next few days of
Scott-King's life. To even the Comic Muse, the
gadabout, the adventurous one of those heavenly
sisters, to whom so little that is human comes amiss,

85

who can mix in almost any company and find a
welcome at almost every door—even to her there
are forbidden places.   Let us leave Scott-King then
on the high seas and meet him again as, sadly
changed, he comes at length into harbour.   The
hatches are off, the August sun seems cool and
breathless, Mediterranean air fresh and spring-like
as at length he climbs on deck.   There are soldiers ;
there is barbed wire ;   there is a waiting lorry ;
there is a drive through a sandy landscape, more
soldiers, more wire.   All the time Scott-King is in
a daze.   He is first fully conscious in a tent, sitting
stark naked while a man in khaki drill taps his
knee with a ruler.

   ' I say, Doc, I know this man.'   He looks up
into a vaguely familiar face.   ' You *are* Mr. Scott-
King, aren't you ?   What on earth are you doing
with this bunch, sir ? '

   ' Lockwood !   Good gracious, you used to be in
my Greek set !   Where am I ? '

   ' No. 64 Jewish Illicit Immigrants' Camp,
Palestine.'

   Granchester reassembled in the third week of
September.   On the first evening of term, Scott-
King sat in the masters' common-room and half
heard Griggs telling of his trip abroad.   ' It gives

one a new angle to things, getting out of England for a bit. What did you do, Scottie?'

'Oh, nothing much. I met Lockwood. You remember him. Sad case, he was a sitter for the Balliol scholarship. Then he had to go into the army.'

'I thought he was still in it. How typical of old Scottie that all he has to tell us after eight weeks away is that he met a prize pupil! I shouldn't be surprised to hear you did some work, too, you old blackleg.'

'To tell you the truth I feel a little *désœuvré*. I must look for a new subject.'

'You've come to the end of old Bellorius at last?'

'Quite to the end.'

Later the headmaster sent for Scott-King.

'You know,' he said, 'we are starting this year with fifteen fewer classical specialists than we had last term?'

'I thought that would be about the number.'

'As you know I'm an old Greats man myself. I deplore it as much as you do. But what are we to do? Parents are not interested in producing the " complete man " any more. They want to qualify their boys for jobs in the modern world. You can hardly blame them, can you?'

' Oh yes,' said Scott-King. ' I can and do.'

' I always say you are a much more important man here than I am. One couldn't conceive of Granchester without Scott-King. But has it ever occurred to you that a time may come when there will be no more classical boys at all ? '

' Oh yes. Often.'

' What I was going to suggest was——I wonder if you will consider taking some other subject as well as the classics ? History, for example, preferably economic history ? '

' No, headmaster.'

' But, you know, there may be something of a crisis ahead.'

' Yes, headmaster.'

' Then what do you intend to do ? '

' If you approve, headmaster, I will stay as I am here as long as any boy wants to read the classics. I think it would be very wicked indeed to do anything to fit a boy for the modern world.'

' It's a short-sighted view, Scott-King.'

' There, headmaster, with all respect, I differ from you profoundly. I think it the most long-sighted view it is possible to take.'

Stinchcombe, 1946

88

COMPOSED IN MONOTYPE WALBAUM AND
PRINTED BY R. & R. CLARK, LTD., EDINBURGH